D0596025

THE YETI FILES

Attack of the Kraken

KEVIN SHERRY

This one is dedicated to your teachers.
They care about you more than you can imagine.

ISBN 978-1-338-13156-7

12 11 10 9 8 7 6 5 4 3 2 1   16 17 18 19 20 21

Printed in the U.S.A.   40

First Scholastic paperback printing, October 2016

Book design by Carol Ly

THE YETI FILES

Attack of the Kraken

KEVIN SHERRY

SCHOLASTIC INC.

Thanks to Mom, Dad, Brian, Teresa Kietlinski, Devlin Rice, Patrick Raube, Valeska Populoh, Michael Lamason, Katherine Fahey, Carlyn Thomas, Matt Gemmel, Ed Schrader, Dan Deacon, Bucketlist, Emily Wexler, Bun Magic Pro Tour, Remington, and Baltimore.

Chapter 1:
A PECULIAR PET

Gunthar! Alex! Come inside.

The Cryptosub is fixed. It's almost time to take it on our next mission!

You see that over there? That's Alexander and Gunthar's igloo.

They love playing in it. But they always end up arguing.

I say, let goblins and elves be goblins and elves!

I'll just give them a little more time out here.

You won't be able to keep it a secret from Blizz forever. And anyway, it's super dangerous.

That thing is a wild animal. You can't tame it.

SQUAWK!

Chapter 2:
TRAVEL BY SUB

Hey, guys!

Frank and I got the new and improved **Cryptosub** up and running.

SONAR
GIZMO

JET THRUSTERS

HIGH-SPEED
PROPELLER

ROBOT ARMS

Anyway, if you read

The Yeti Files #2:
Monsters on the Run,

you will remember that we
got an urgent alert from the
merfolk of Atlantis.

CLANK!

SHAMELESS
PLUG

OVER IT.

You may have heard of **mermaids**— half fish, half ladies. Real merfolk are people who have spent so much time in the water, they have adapted to living in it all of the time.

MERFOLK SWIMMING GEAR

WEBBED GLOVES

SLEEK TAIL

STYLISH FASHION SENSE

Like fish, merfolk have gills so they can breathe underwater. But like people, they can also use their mouths—and their legs! Most merfolk prefer to wear a tail, though. It's just way cooler!

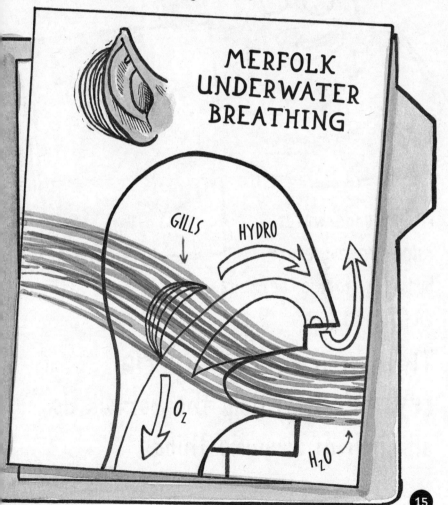

MERFOLK UNDERWATER BREATHING

GILLS

HYDRO

O_2

H_2O

The merfolk live in the lost city of Atlantis.

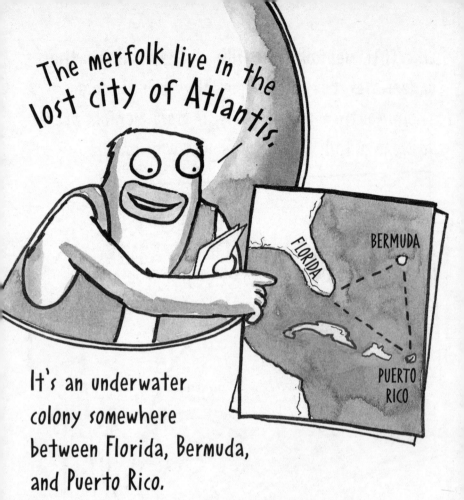

It's an underwater colony somewhere between Florida, Bermuda, and Puerto Rico.

The area is rich with **special crystals** that help the merfolk do all kinds of awesome things.

Crystal technology powers their cities, grows their food, and produces everything they need. It also can make anything disappear, including socks, homework, and human ships that stray into the so-called Bermuda Triangle. We'll travel there to answer their call for help.

To get to Atlantis, we'll go down through the underwater air lock here in my lair.

Its tunnel leads to the Indian Ocean.

UNDERWATER AIR LOCK

INDIAN OCEAN

From there, we travel past Australia (G'day, mate!), swing by Hawaii (Aloha!), and finally arrive at the Bermuda Triangle.

Pack a good book, boys.
It's going to be a long trip!

Chapter 3:
MEET THE MAYOR

I hear Atlantis has this great new mayor. He's sending a team to meet us, so we can't be late.

Take a deep breath,
hold on tight, and
don't lose your lunch.

It's go time!

We're so happy you are here.

When the attacks began, we didn't know who else to call. The kraken will not let us live in peace.

The mayor is madder than an octopus with its arms tied.

The mayor is right this way.

He's just finishing a meeting with his supporters. They are so proud of how he's helped our city grow.

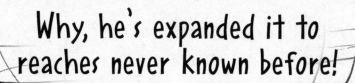

Ah, yes. Blizz Richards! Good trip? Yes, yes, well let's get straight to more important matters . . . **me.**

I have a lot of power in this town, of course. Not to brag, but I was elected with the greatest majority of all time. **But with that power comes great responsibility.**

Atlantis was always a fine city, mind you. But under my leadership it has become truly extraordinary.

I was the first to harness the true power of our crystals.

As a young boy,
I studied our crystals carefully.
They power everything in our lives.

Soon I was using them to create **great vehicles** and **industrial machines**. I even perfected a **force field** that shields us from the world above the waves.

And now I'm using crystal power to build a **brighter, better Atlantis.**

Which means we must constantly mine the sea for more crystals!

But our whole way of life is being threatened by a **terrible monster!**

SEA TURTLE

GIANT SQUID

BARRACUDA

SQUID

TERRIBLE MONSTER

This damage could only have
been done by the kraken.
Look at how big the suction marks are!

You must find the kraken and **stop him!**

My trusty security team will help you get started.

You'll need ID, registration, and temporary water insurance. And we'll have to get you all fitted for tails. But first let's go over our Atlantis bylaws:

Law #1: Don't feed the sharks.

Law #2: Never swim alone in a dark alley.

Law #3: Littering the ocean is never allowed.

Law #4: Never interfere with crystal technology.

...e crossing a waterway.

Chapter 4:
NEW FRIENDS

I'm glad we snuck outta there.

We have work to do!

But before Blizz and the team could begin, they were accosted by an excited young mermaid with eyes that looked rather . . . *intense.*

Blizz Richards! This is a dream come true. My name is Coral and I am a megafan. I have a scrapbook of all your famous cases. I need to talk to you desperately!

Mayor Blacksand is not all he seems to be.

Yes, Atlantis has changed under his leadership— but it's not all *good* news.

He has convinced the merfolk that crystals are the only way to make our lives better.

39

Crystals have always been important to us.

They power our cities, but they are also the heart of the sea itself. Without them, the ocean and all who live here cannot survive.

But Blacksand only wants them so he can expand the city—and his power over it. All he cares about is crystals, **crystals, crystals!**

And now he's using them to make **bigger machines** to dig out **bigger crystals.**

He is **obsessed!**

He has convinced our people with his impressive technology that **we deserve to own all crystals.**

"What do I think of Blacksand? His crystal-powered Internet is the best. My video game screen has never been clearer."

"He has created so many jobs. My son Barnacle is out there driving a forklift . . . and finally off my couch."

"I give his fireworks displays **two thumbs up.** Those crystals can really blow things sky-high!"

"Hasn't anyone noticed that the more the mayor builds, the more the kraken attacks us?"

45

ALERT!
KRAKEN ATTACK
Blacksand here!
We will not stand for these attacks. No one in Atlantis will become another Emily Airwalker.

She became interested in the myth of the kraken and hoped to one day see the beast with her own eyes.

And so she went looking for it. She would be gone for months at a time, and then one day she disappeared completely.

ATLANTIS HISTORY

Blacksand blames the kraken.

ATLANTIS TIMES
AIRWALKER MISSING!

49

Chapter 5:
DETECTIVE WORK

Speaking of disappearing, I wonder where Frank has gone off to. Can you guys go find him?

Oh, no . . .

We got this!

While Alexander and Gunthar were arguing—again—Coral was leading Blizz to the Museum of Atlantis.

It's the finest museum in the world.

They have collections of the best pieces of both human and cryptid history, art, and science.

The exhibit about Emily Airwalker has lots of information about her life and her search for the kraken.

Hopefully we'll find something useful.

ANCIENT COLUMN

PIECE OF THE GREAT WALL OF ATLANTIS

ORB OF POSEIDON

MERFOLK MASTERPIECES

Slow down!

FIRST AQUA CAR

Nope!

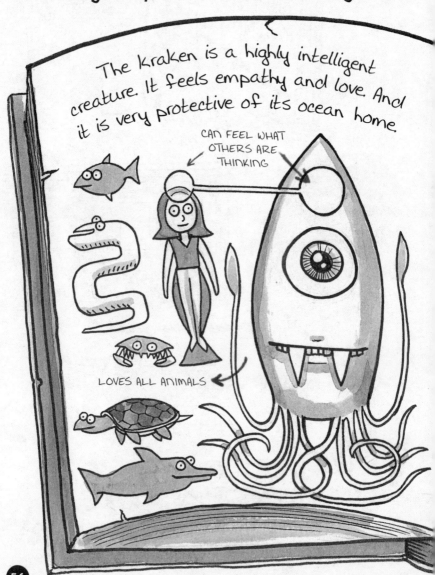

The kraken is a highly intelligent creature. It feels empathy and love. And it is very protective of its ocean home.

CAN FEEL WHAT OTHERS ARE THINKING

LOVES ALL ANIMALS

they looked for clues in Emily's journal.

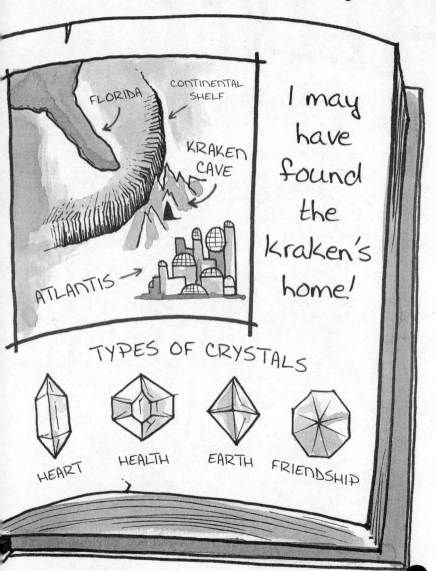

FLORIDA

CONTINENTAL SHELF

KRAKEN CAVE

ATLANTIS

I may have found the kraken's home!

TYPES OF CRYSTALS

HEART   HEALTH   EARTH   FRIENDSHIP

We've got to find the kraken before Blacksand does.

Hopefully the map in Emily's journal will lead us to it!

Chapter 6:
ALEX AND GUNTHAR ARE DOIN' FINE

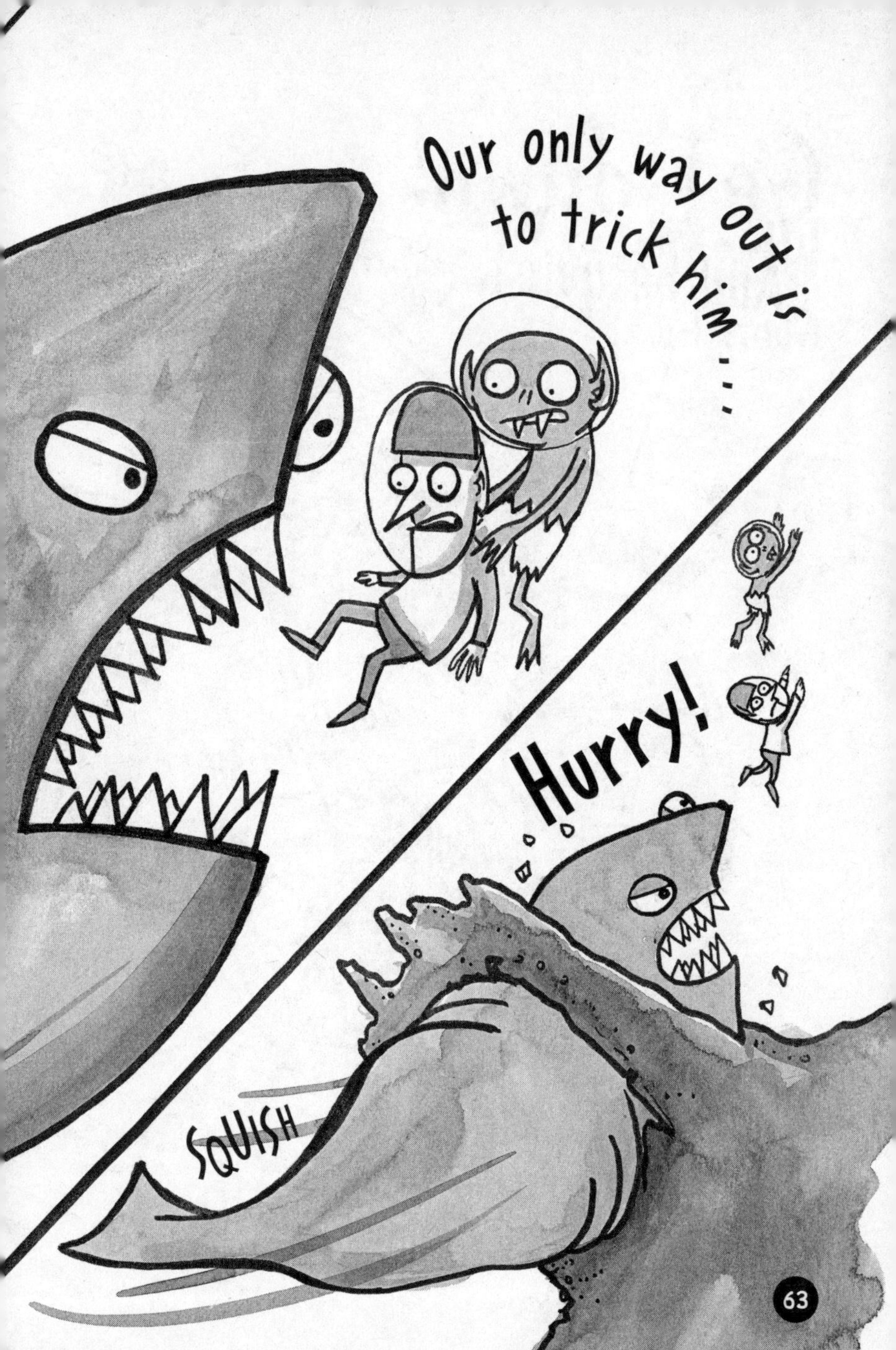
Our only way out is to trick him . . .
Hurry!
SQUISH

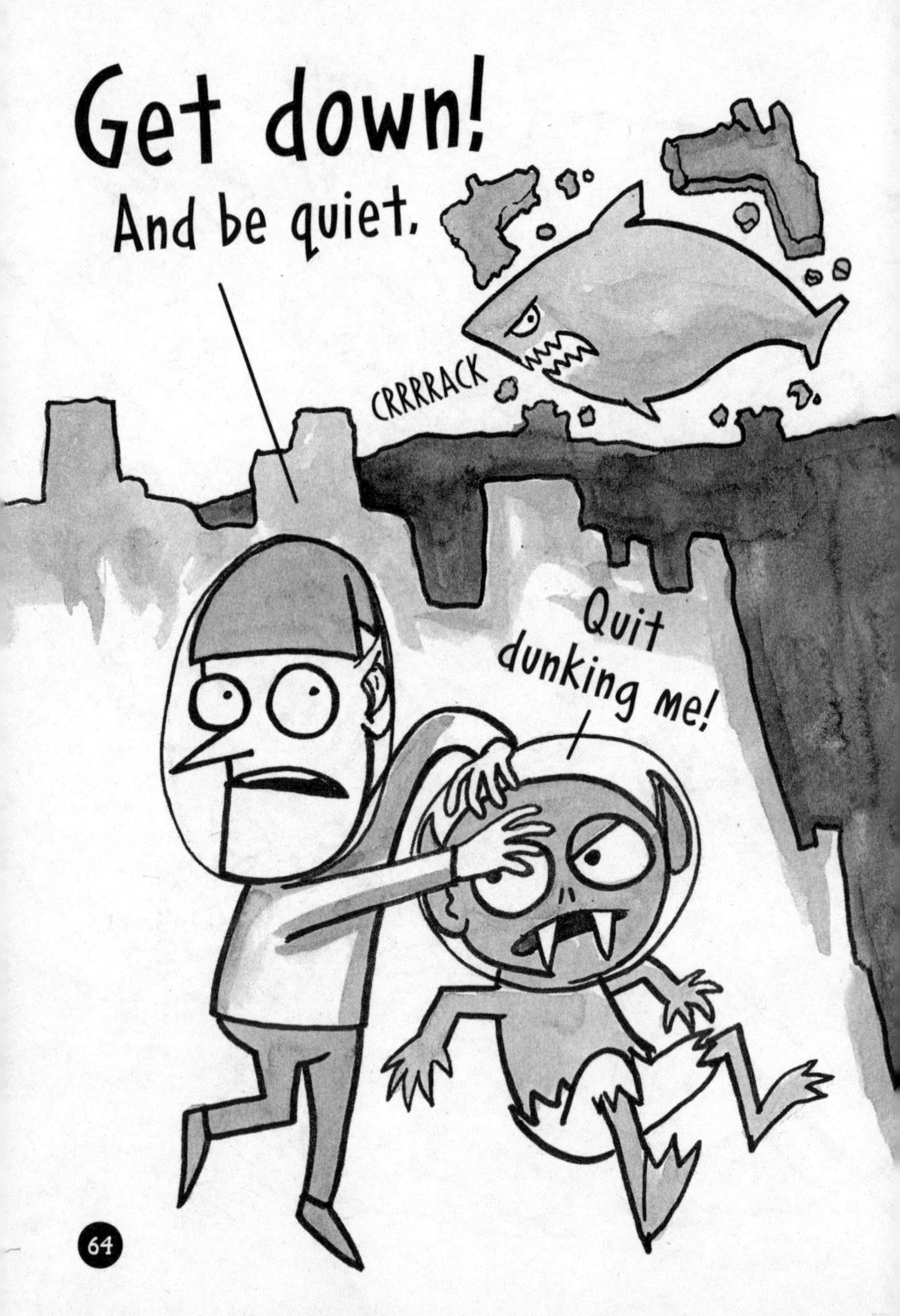
Get down!
And be quiet.
CRRRRACK
Quit dunking me!

Meanwhile . . .

Frank was making a new friend—as always.

Dolphins love to explore.

And see old pals.

This guy knows cool tricks.

Hello, there!

Told you!

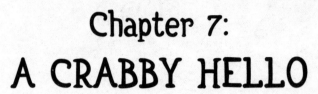

Chapter 7:
A CRABBY HELLO

Blizz and Coral had almost reached the cave Emily had written about.

We passed the trench and turned right at the reef.

We should be getting close...

Hey! Do you see that?

Those are **flying goggles**, not **swimming goggles**. Could Emily have left them behind all those years ago?

Down here, Coral.

I see the cave. But I'm not sure how we're going to get inside.

Where do you two think you're going?
This cave is secret.

The kraken says so.
Wait ... I wasn't
supposed to tell anyone
about the kraken!
No matter, soon you won't
be able to tell anyone.

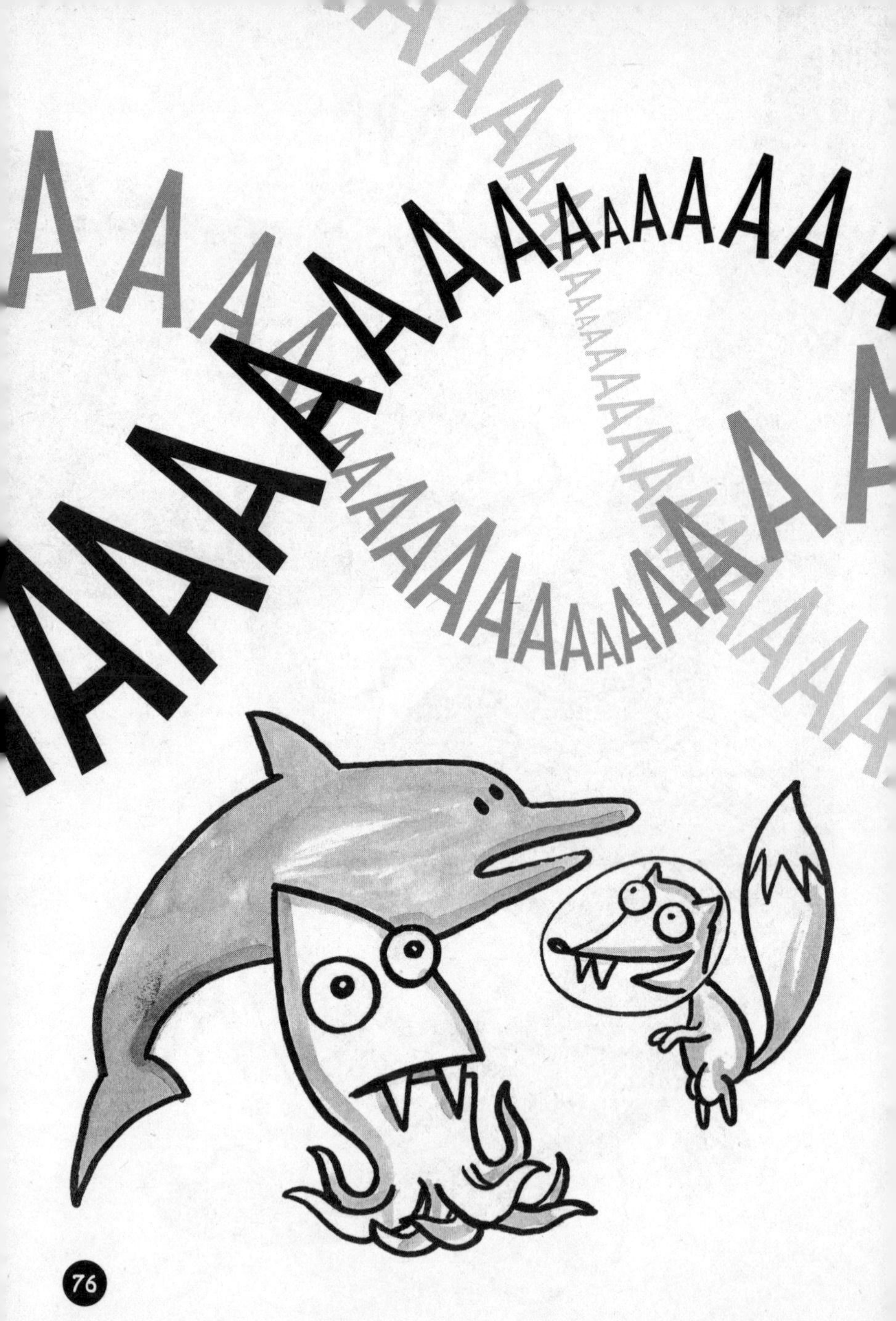

AAAAAAAAAAAAAAAAAAAAAAAAAAAAAAAAAAAAAA
That's my friend, Blizz!
Don't worry! I know how to handle that big bully.

This drippy, disgusting fish head is his favorite snack.
Gimme!
Gimme!

And so Blizz and Coral snuck into the cave.

I didn't really want to eat that furry white guy anyway!

NOM NOM NOM

Chapter 8:
TRUTH IN THE DEEP

ORGANIC KELP FARM

It's the kraken!
And look who else...

SEA MONKEY HOUSE

SLEEPING POD

MINIONS

BREAKFAST NOOK

EMILY AIRWALKER

HEART STONE

Emily Airwalker! You're alive.
We've learned so much about you and your research!
What do you mean?

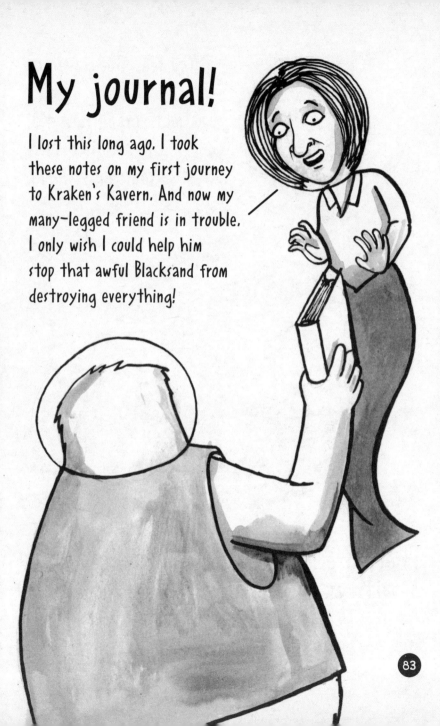

My journal!

I lost this long ago. I took these notes on my first journey to Kraken's Kavern. And now my many-legged friend is in trouble. I only wish I could help him stop that awful Blacksand from destroying everything!

You see, the mayor of Atlantis doesn't understand how the magic of the sea really works.

There are many kinds of crystals, with many different powers.

They inspire scientific discovery, art, music, food, love, and friendship.

And the most important crystal of all, the **Heart Stone**, keeps the oceans alive and creates harmony around the world.

The mighty kraken is responsible for protecting it from falling into the wrong hands.

I have always allowed the merfolk to take some of the **krystals** to power Atlantis and so they may live **kalmly** and **kontentedly.**

But Mayor Blacksand has gotten greedy!

He has mined too many **krystals**, and that has weakened the **krust** of our **kavern**. If he doesn't stop, the **kavern** will **krack**.

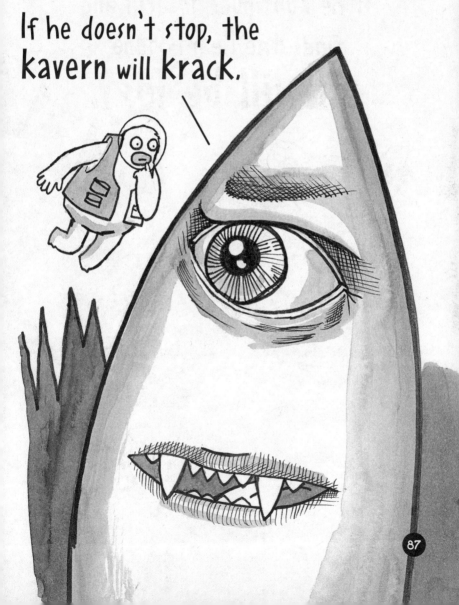

I'm scared, Blizz Richards.

If he kontinues to drill and finds the Heart Stone, **all will be lost.**

Who knows what damage he might do with
a krystal as powerful as the Heart Stone!

So my minions and I have done what we had to do to kancel his plans.

We would never hurt a living kreature.

Yet we have tried to krush Blacksand's konstruction projects.

But only to protect the Heart Stone. We would much rather help our fellow kreatures.

Ha-ha-ha! This drill is my greatest invention. Soon I'll have so many crystals, I'll be elected mayor-for-life!

Just when Blacksand's luck was running out . . .

We'll save you!

But first . . .
where are my
crystals?

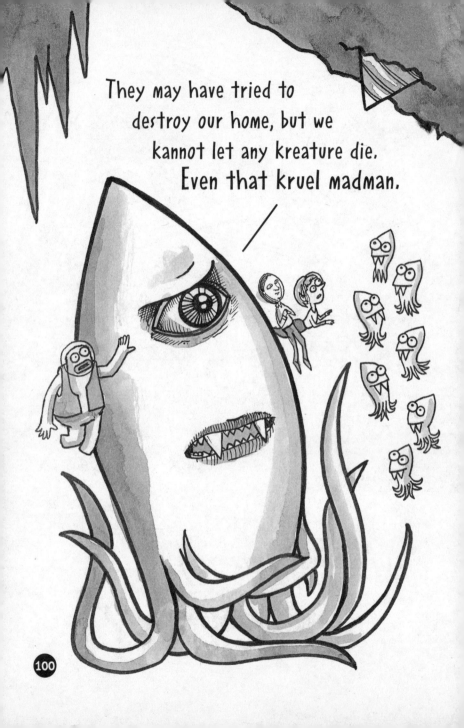

They may have tried to destroy our home, but we kannot let any kreature die. Even that kruel madman.

And so the mermen were saved!

Have you ever thought about a career in security?

Thank you!

Mayor Blacksand was arrested and taken to City Hall to answer for his crimes.

Chapter 10:
FRESH SEAFOOD

....

Gunthar and Alexander were still hopelessly lost.

RECIPES
FOR
EATING
PEOPLE

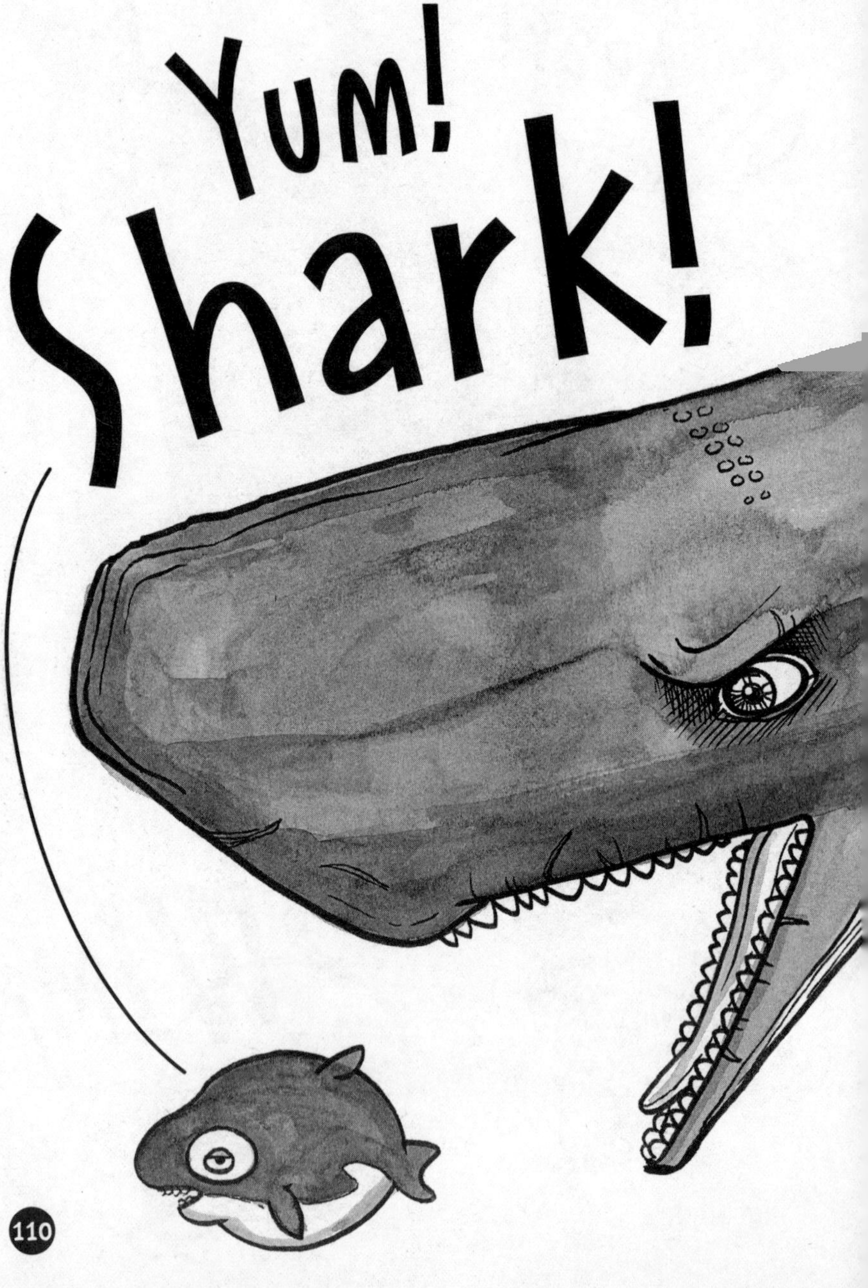
Yum! Shark!

Can you believe that just happened?!

I'm not going to say I told you so. But I told you that wild animals are dangerous.

And so Alex and Gunthar escaped the food chain.

I give up! Frank is on his own.

Let's go find Blizz.

Chapter 11:
A NEW ATLANTIS

Back at City Hall, a new council was elected to rule Atlantis.

We, the council, sentence you, Julius Blacksand, to one year of hard labor fixing Kraken's Kavern. And you will spend the full year **without your tail!**

No tail?

This council has decided to replace the old laws with three new ones.

Law #1: Take care of the ocean.
Law #2: Respect all creatures.
Law #3: Listen to your sister!

Chapter 12:
TROUBLE IN THE AIR

Whew! I'm going to put my feet up for a bit...

Uh, Blizz?

Jack Saturday is waiting for you on the Cryptotron.

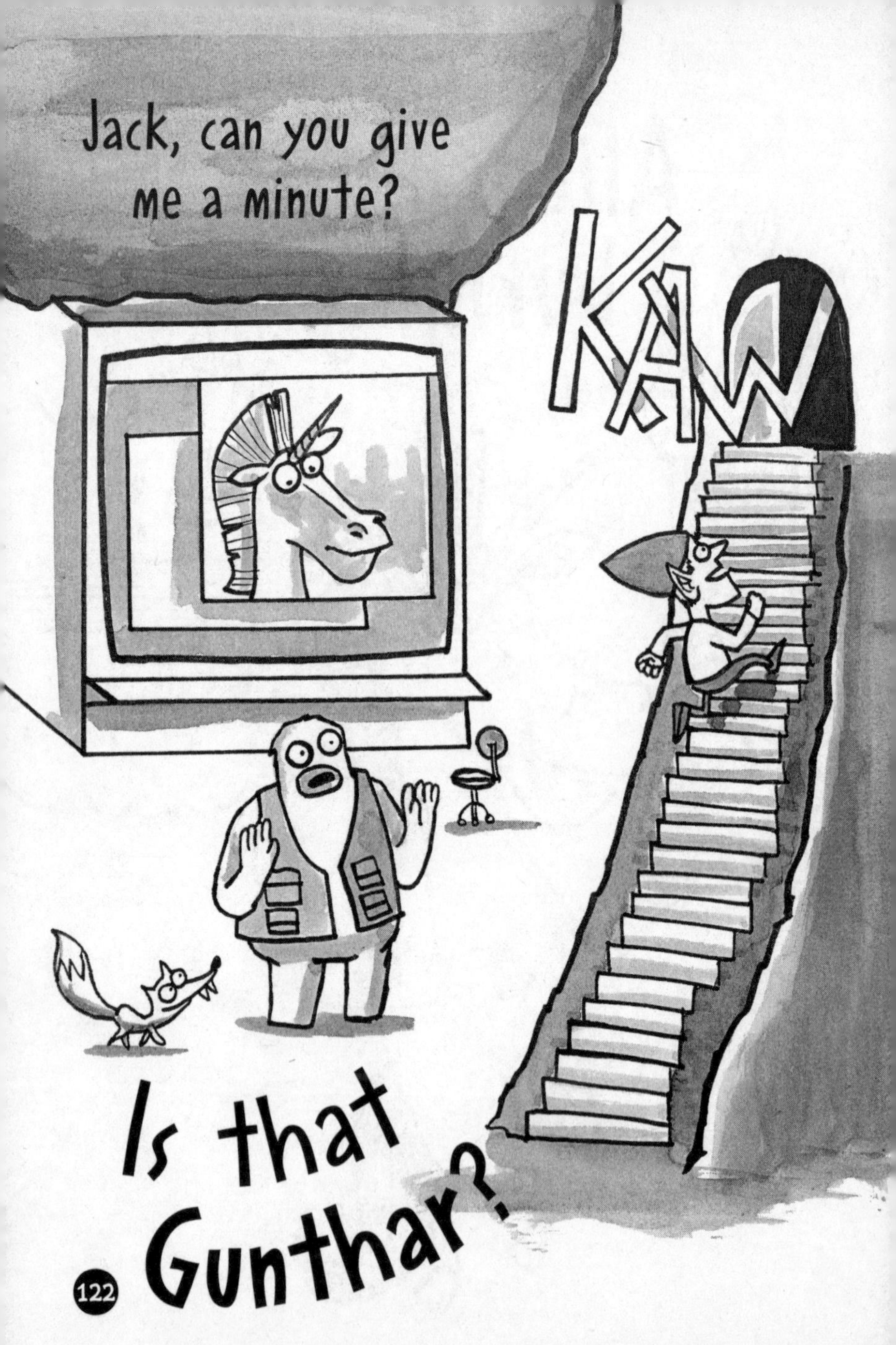
Jack, can you give me a minute?
KAW
Is that Gunthar?